SLIGHTLY SPOOKY STORIES

Did You Hear Something?

Written by
Michael Teitelbaum

Illustrated by
Pat Stewart

kidsbooks®
Incorporated

Copyright © 1992 Kidsbooks Inc. and Michael Teitelbaum
Illustrations Copyright © Pat Stewart

Kidsbooks Inc.
7004 N. California Ave.
Chicago, IL 60645

In the small town of Beaver Falls, the school wilderness club was having its annual camping weekend. The five regular members of the club were going, along with five campers from a nearby town.

Mr. Terry, the teacher in charge of the club, was leading the campers into the woods.

"Looks like we have a few more kids than last year," said eight-year-old Becky, president of the club.

"Yeah," said nine-year-old Troy, the club's vice-president, with a devilish gleam in his eye. "The more kids, the better the scary story is!"

After about two hours of hiking, the group finally reached the Beaver Falls campsite.

"This is it, gang!" yelled Becky. "We're here!"

Everyone was glad to stop hiking and take off their packs. With Mr. Terry's help, the children took the next hour to set up their tents.

Dinner was cooked over an open campfire, and soon the tired campers had slipped into their tents for the night.

At least, that was what they thought!

When the full moon had risen to its peak in the night sky and he was sure that Mr. Terry was asleep, Troy slipped over to Becky's tent. "Ready?" he whispered.

"Yep," answered Becky. "Let's get the others."

Troy and Becky went from tent to tent, quietly waking the other campers. Soon, all the kids were in Troy's tent—the tent that was farthest from Mr. Terry.

"Are you going to tell us a scary story?" asked seven-year-old Kyle, who loved scary stories.

"I'm going to tell you the Legend of Beaver Falls," began Troy. "Legend has it that something weird lives out in these woods!"

Nervous laughter spread through the tent, as campers huddled close together.

Troy continued. "Late at night, deep in the woods, it is said that you can hear the sounds of a strange creature. This mysterious creature has three legs, huge wings, and makes an eerie, high-pitched, whistling sound. Anyone who has ever heard these sounds will never forget them!"

The sound of footsteps interrupted Troy.
"Did you hear something?" asked Kyle.
The footsteps came again. *Step, step, step,* then a pause. *Step, step, STEP!* and again a pause. Then, one more time, the three-step pattern was repeated.

Next, a high-pitched whistle filled the air, followed closely by the flapping of wings.

"The creature!" whispered Kyle.

Troy and Becky looked at each other. This story had been told in Beaver Falls for years. Becky first heard it from her older brother. But it was just a story. No one had ever really heard the sounds. They were just trying to have a little fun, and keep the legend alive.

But now, Troy and Becky were scared themselves!

"Come on, Troy," said Becky, mustering all her courage. "Let's go check this out."

"Everybody stay here," ordered Troy. "It's okay. Mr. Terry is sleeping right over in that tent. If you see anything, wake him up."

Becky and Troy made their way through the dense, dark woods, guided only by the narrow beams of their flashlights.

Suddenly Becky heard a twig snap behind her and felt a hand grab her shoulder.

"Yaaaa!" she yelled, turning in shock.

There stood Kyle. "Sorry," he said sheepishly. "I didn't mean to frighten you. I just love scary stuff, and I didn't want to miss out on the fun, so I followed you."

Becky caught her breath, and the three children moved on into the woods.

"Did you hear something?" asked Becky a short while later.

Step, step, step, came the sounds. Then a whistle and the flapping of wings.

"It's behind us!" shouted Troy, dashing away from the sounds.

"Troy, it's following us!" cried Becky. Every turn they made, the creature was right behind them.

"We're lost!" exclaimed Troy.

"Lost in the woods with that thing after us!" cried Kyle. The sounds came again, and the children kept running.

They came upon a clearing in the woods. There, in the middle of the clearing, stood a log cabin. Smoke curled from its chimney.

"It looks like someone's home!" said Becky, fighting back the panic.

"Come on," said Troy. "Maybe we can get some help in there!"

The three campers burst into the cabin, out of breath, and slammed the door behind them. There, sitting peacefully near a blazing fireplace, was an old man.

"Mister, you've got to help us!" cried Troy nervously.

"Yeah," continued Kyle, "there's a creature in the woods chasing us. He's headed this way!"

"Have a seat," the old man said calmly.

"But you don't understand," said Becky excitedly. "There's a creature with three legs and big wings and—"

"Whoa, whoa," interrupted the old man, raising his wrinkled hand. "Slow down, young lady. I assure you there's nothing to be afraid of."

There was no sound outside now except for the forest crickets. The three campers sat down and began to relax.

"Who are you?" asked Becky.

"Well, you might call me a nature lover," began the old man. "For the past 50 years I've lived in the woods. I grow food and flowers, and I've made friends with many of the animals."

The man got up, grabbed his heavy wooden cane and walked to the door. *Step, step, STEP!* he went.

"There's your creature!" said Troy in an excited whisper. "His cane makes the third step."

"I'd like you to meet a friend of mine," said the man. He opened his door and whistled.

"The whistle!" whispered Becky.

A few seconds later they heard the flapping of wings. A big owl came flying over to the old man, landing right on his arm.

"There's your terrible winged creature!" said Becky a bit too loudly.

"I'm afraid that Hooter here is the only terrible winged creature you'll find in these woods," said the old man. "I'm sorry if he frightened you."

The three campers were embarrassed. They told the man about the legend. He let out a big laugh.

"People are always afraid of what they don't understand," he said. "So you came here in search of a terrible creature, huh? Well, I'm sorry to disappoint you."

"No, sir," said Becky. "We're not disappointed. It's very nice to meet you, but we should be getting back to our camp. The others will start to worry."

"I'd rather the whole world didn't find out about my little cabin here," said the old man.

"Don't worry," said Troy. "Your secret is safe with us."

"I'm pretty tired," said the old man. "I'm going to turn in for the night. But come back and visit some time," he added, waving goodbye.

The three campers disappeared into the woods, heading back to their camp.

Back at camp, the others were frantic with worry. Becky, Troy, and Kyle burst from the trees scaring the daylights out of most of the campers.

"What did you find?" everyone wanted to know, as they gathered around the three returning campers.

"Well," began Becky, "we caught a glimpse of the creature, but it darted off into the woods before we could get close enough for a really good look."

"Did it have three legs?" asked one camper.

"And big, ugly wings?" asked another.

"We think so," answered Troy. "But we may never know. Now, I think we should all go to sleep. The creature won't bother us anymore tonight." Troy felt good that he not only kept the legend alive, but was able to protect his new friend's privacy, as well.

As the campers stretched out in their tents, the sound of footsteps once again broke through the night.

Troy dashed to Becky's tent. "Did you hear something?" he asked.

Before she could answer, the unmistakable *Step, Step, STEP!* followed by the whistling and flapping of wings caused heads to pop out of all the tents in camp.

"If the old man is sleeping in his cabin," started Troy.

"Then who's making that noise?" finished Becky.

All the campers, including Troy and Becky, slipped back into their tents, zipping the flaps tightly, and hiding deep inside their sleeping bags.

What they didn't see was an old woman, the old man's wife, walking past their camp. She too walked with a heavy wooden cane, and whistled to call the pet owl she shared with her husband.